Shirley Hughes

LUCY & TOM

At Christmas

In loving memory of Sally

LUCY AND TOM AT CHRISTMAS
A RED FOX BOOK 978 1 782 95550 4

First published in Great Britain by Victor Gollancz, 1981
Published in Picture Puffins, 1985

This edition published by Red Fox, an imprint of Random House Children's Publishers UK
A Penguin Random House Company

Penguin
Random House
UK

This edition published 2015

1 3 5 7 9 10 8 6 4 2

Penguin Random House is committed to a sustainable future for our business, our readers and our planet.
This book is made from Forest Stewardship Council® certified paper.

MIX
Paper from
responsible sources
FSC
www.fsc.org
FSC® C018179

Red Fox Books are published by Random House Children's Publishers UK,
61–63 Uxbridge Road, London W5 5SA

www.randomhousechildrens.co.uk
www.randomhouse.co.uk

Addresses for companies within The Random House Group Limited
can be found at: www.randomhouse.co.uk/offices.htm

THE RANDOM HOUSE GROUP Limited Reg. No. 954009

A CIP catalogue record for this book is available from the British Librar

Printed in China

Christmas is coming! Lucy and Tom
are helping to stir the Christmas pudding.
As they stir they each make a wish.

The postman comes to the house more often than usual. He brings cards wishing them all a merry Christmas, and sometimes parcels too. These have to be hidden away until Christmas Day comes.

Lucy and Tom are making their own Christmas cards
with pictures of robins and Christmas trees on them.

They've made some paper chains too,
to make the house look pretty.
Mum is putting up some green leaves.

On the hall table they've put a crib with Mary and Joseph and Baby Jesus, the three kings, the shepherds, and a donkey and a cow. Lucy and Tom have cut out a big gold paper star to hang over them and put pretend cotton-wool snow all around.

They have presents for everybody in the family. Lucy has:

A sparkly brooch for Mum.

A rubber in the shape of a dog
for Dad to take to his office.

A comb in a case for Granny
with A for Alison on it
(because that's Granny's name).

A handkerchief for Grandpa
with J for John on it
(because that's Grandpa's name).

And a shiny blue car for Tom.

Tom has:

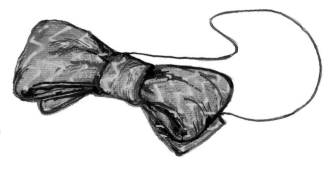

A mug for Mum to have her tea out of.

A smart bow-tie on an elastic for Dad.

A calendar for Granny which he made at nursery school.

A packet of seeds for Grandpa to grow flowers from when the spring comes.

And a pen for Lucy which changes into different colours.

Lucy and Tom have wrapped up their presents already. Tom hides his in a different place every day. And every day he asks Lucy to guess what her present is going to be.

They talk a lot about the presents they hope they're going to get for Christmas.

Mum helps them both to write letters to Father Christmas and post them up the chimney.

There's a knock at the door. Some big children have come to sing carols.

One afternoon a band comes to their street to play
Christmas music. Lucy and Tom run out to watch.
They know some of the tunes. They can sing *Silent Night*,
Away in a Manger and *Once in Royal David's City*.

Lucy and Tom go to the market with Dad to choose a Christmas tree. There are crowds of people. The lights are shining out and the shops and stalls are full of exciting things.

Christmas Eve has come at last. Dad gets home early, and together they hang all sorts of pretty glittering things on the tree. Then they arrange the parcels underneath it.

Now it's bedtime. Lucy and Tom hang up their stockings at the
end of their beds. They look out at the sky. It's beginning to snow.
Mum says, "Good, it's going to be a white Christmas."
Lucy and Tom are *far* too excited to go to sleep. How can
you get to sleep when Father Christmas may be coming?

But somehow or other they do. When they wake
up it's very early and still dark. It's Christmas Day.
Has Father Christmas come? Yes, he has!
Lucy and Tom feel into their stockings and pull
out the presents one by one.

Lucy and Tom go along to Mum and Dad's room to show them what Father Christmas has brought. But it's a bit too soon for them yet. Imagine not wanting to wake up early on Christmas Day! Lucy and Tom go back to their room and play with their new toys.

Now Mum and Dad
have woken up.
They all hug each
other. Christmas has
really begun.

After breakfast they look out. It's white everywhere and very cold. But the sun comes out as they walk to church.

When they are at home again lots of people arrive – Granny and Grandpa, Granny's old friend Mrs Barlow who lives all by herself, Aunty Jill and Uncle Rob and their little baby, Elizabeth. That's ten people for dinner. Everyone helps to get it ready.

They all sit down round the table to eat roast turkey, Christmas pudding and lots of other delicious things. Afterwards they pull crackers. There are some loud bangs, but Mrs Barlow doesn't mind a bit. She says she doesn't hear as well as she used to, and she just smiles and smiles.

After everything is cleared away, Lucy and Tom
give out a present for everyone from underneath
the tree. What a lot of surprises!

Elizabeth only likes the wrapping paper
on her present. She goes off to sleep in the
middle of it like a hamster.

Christmas can be quite tiring. Tom gets very
excited about his presents and rather cross.

So he and Grandpa go for a walk together in the snow,
just the two of them. The sun is very big and red.

When they get home again, all the family sit round the fire and play Heads, Bodies and Legs. The first person draws a head and folds over the paper, the next person draws a body, the next person draws some legs and the last person chooses a name. When they're all finished and the papers are opened out, there are some very funny-looking pictures. Lucy calls her person "Uncle Rob" and Tom calls his "Father Christmas". Now it's time to light the tree.

On earth peace, good will toward men.

It's dark outside. The lights shine out into the street. Merry Christmas, Lucy and Tom! Merry Christmas, everyone!